Of Kings and Queens

Tara Kennedy

Copyright

Table of Contents

Author Notes

FOR THE HAWAIIAN USED here, Hawaiian typically makes use of the kahako or the macron to indicate emphasis. Screen and ereaders are not great at rendering those, so I opted to skip them. I understand that this can make the Hawaiian more difficult to read for Hawaiian speakers.

Also for the very brief use of Japanese, I chose to use romaji for similar reasons.

And on a separate note, there is reference to parental divorce here.

Chapter 1

Jia Mei Chapman hated being late. She rushed out of her door and bumped into a guy standing there. She said, "Sorry" and tried to move around him.

"Chapman?" he said, holding out a package.

"Yeah." She accepted the box, scrawled a signature on his tablet, and raced down the stairs. Racing was a mistake because the summer DC humidity was really showing itself off today. She arrived at So Sakura a sweaty mess. She came in through the back kitchen, waving to the cooks, and sticking her stuff including the box into the cubby. She raced to the bathroom to splash some water on her wrists. Her dark hair was already trying to frizz up just enough to be annoying. Being Hawaiian, Chinese, Irish, and German, she was never sure which of her heritages to blame for frizz.

The hostess stand was right under an AC vent and the new air filter. She'd be an ice cube in about twenty minutes, but at least she'd look like a contained ice cube.

"Kon'nichiwa, Jia," her boss Tony said bowing to her.

Jia bowed back.

The restaurant's position near the Mall and several hotels meant they trafficked a lot in tourists. Tony believed the appearance of them speaking in Japanese helped create the authentic experience tourists craved. Jia had offered to take Japanese if Tony would pay for the class, but he had said there was no need. He spoke enough Japanese for the both of them.

Jia carried on to the hostess stand. She took a look at the reservations and currently occupied tables. Tony had once again, not entered half the tables he sat. This was the reason she hated being late. Tony was half-hazard with the software, no matter how many times she explained to him that the software let them create reports and track statistics, but it only worked if they filled in all the tables.

She picked up the tablet and started scanning the restaurant to figure out which tables were missing.

When she went to collect her stuff after they closed, she saw the package. The box was small and easy enough to carry in one hand. She turned to Carrie, one of the waitresses.

"What day is it?" Jia asked. After a day of sorting reservations, she should have remembered. She pictured the reservation screen in her head.

Carrie glanced up. "Huh? It's Thursday."

"It's June," Jia said. "Dammit."

"Forget to pay your rent or something?"

Jia had a direct deposit set up for that with her landlord. The tourist season lulled a bit after cherry blossom/spring break season, but picked back up with college graduations and Memorial Day weekend. Jia had been busy dealing with guests, the large reservations, and surviving the increase in walk-ins, calls, and emails. So she had forgotten.

"It's fine, it's just my family." Jia looked back at the box. She wanted to shake it. Her parents' acrimonious divorce had turned into something that called for six kinds of lawyers and a news making trademark case. But neither of them had ever sent dangerous packages.

"I thought you didn't talk to your family." Carrie leaned in to look at the package.

"Yeah," Jia said, though it was more complicated. Jia had only been able to afford therapy for three months before the pandemic restaurant closure made therapy a luxury. But the therapist had told Jia she had fallen into a trap of trying to mediate her parents' relationship. That Jia could not fix their behavioral patterns, only her own.

Her mom's restaurant closed for one holiday a year, no matter what day of the week it fell on. King Kamehameha Day fell on June eleventh every year. While the Native Hawaiian population in DC was smaller than in some areas of the mainland, there were enough folks that combined with the various people who had been stationed for one reason or another in Hawai'i and missed it, Kamehameha Day gathered up a crowd.

The first year after her dad had opened his own restaurant named Kou Keiki - now known as Na Keiki, he had tried to invite a bunch of family friends to come to his restaurant for an after-party of sorts. That had been the first year Jia refused to talk to either of her parents on Kamehameha Day. After that, her dad's restaurant decided on staying open, doing a big business giving out plastic lei and half-price pineapple drinks.

"Do you want me to open it?" Carrie asked.

Jia looked at the box. She undid the tape on the bottom and slid the box top off. It was a flower. Well, several floral things. She lifted it out to see the flowers were attached to a hair clip. A card rested underneath. It said, "Don't forget, it goes on the right since you are still single. -Mom"

"Thanks, Mom," Jia said.

"Oh it's a flower," Carrie said. "That's sweet. Ready to go?"

Jia nodded and checked one last time to make sure she hadn't forgotten anything. They moved out into the alley, walking carefully past the dumpsters, onto the sidewalk towards the metro.

"It's not your birthday, right?" Carrie asked.

"No, the flower is for King Kamehameha Day. It's a thing."

"Oh, I think I've heard of him," Carrie said.

Yeah, that was about as much as most people got to. Although, it occurred to Jia that she needed to remind Tony she had the day off and also make sure she ordered some lei.

Chapter 2

Ken followed the sound of laughter past the front kiosk of the florist and through the door to the backroom. "Auntie Diana?"

"Ken, what are you doing here?" Diana looked up from behind a stack of boxes.

He hugged Diana. "Mom said you might need a pair of hands." He held up his hands.

"Oh, your mother. Just because you're scaling back doesn't mean you need to come to help your auntie."

"Well, what can I do?" he asked. He had told his mom he was taking a sabbatical from his mediation program. He had explained many times that this did not mean he had stopped being a lawyer or still didn't have enough work to keep himself occupied. But his mom kept volunteering him for things. She had told him Diana was under the weather and needed reinforcements.

"Can you stand out front? We're almost finished loading up Adriana's car and we have a few pickups coming in today. I don't want to miss anyone."

"Sure."

She kissed his cheek. "All the boxes are labeled in the fridge, but you can call Davey too. Or me."

He smiled. Diana wasn't coughing or anything, but now that he looked closely she did look a little tired. Maybe his mom had been only about eighty percent bullshit.

He sat out front and pulled out his phone.

The door chimed and a whirl of hair came through the door. The dark brown hair picked up glimmers in the light. It topped amazing legs, encased in slim-fit black pants, and a snug black tank top.

The hair flipped back and made him stop even though he already stood still. The face seemed familiar, and he couldn't place it. He felt certain he would have remembered meeting her. But he also felt like he'd been waiting for her somehow.

She spotted him, took a breath, and moved to the kiosk. "Hi." She smiled in a manner that seemed practiced yet warm. "I'm here to pick up an order for Mei - M-e-i."

Mei was such a nice name. She was looking at him. Right, he was supposed to be doing a thing. "Hang on, just a moment and I will check for you." He looked under the kiosk, no boxes there.

He smiled and went to the back room. The back door was still propped open and he could hear voices in the alley. No sign of Davey. He opened the fridge near the door, but the boxes were stuffed in there like a minivan packed for a beach vacation. None of them said Mei in the front row and he was afraid of creating a Jenga pile if he tried to remove any to look behind.

He leaned in the doorframe to the front. "Hang on just a sec," he said to Ms. Mei.

At the back door, he called, "Hey, customer here."

Diana turned back from the front of the van where they appeared to be stuffing even more boxes into the passenger seat.

"Ken, what do you need?"

"Customer," he called, pitched loud enough to be heard over the van's motor.

"Can Davey help you?" she asked.

He held up his hands in the I dunno gesture, because where was Davey?

His aunt sighed. "I'll be back in a sec." She moved around the van door.

"It's fine," Ken said.

His aunt pushed past him to the fridge.

He stood back at the kiosk trying not to stare. "You look so familiar; did you grow up around here?" he asked. Her expression changed to disbelief and he realized how much that sounded like a line. But he also did think she looked familiar. Both things could be true. "I went to Channing," he said. Either she was from here and would recognize the name of the high school, or she wasn't and she would continue thinking he was weird.

"Fitzgerald," she said.

To say Fitzgerald and Channing had a rivalry would imply either school was good at sports. But both schools were regular participants in the local quiz bowl. During Ken's time at the school, the Fitzgerald team kept trouncing the Channing team. He had declined the offer to participate on the Channing team, because he had had no interest in being shown up on local TV like that.

Aunt Diana came back in with a large box. "Sorry for the delay. It's a busy day here today. So, three lei. And I have a note that you were already provided a hairpiece, but we have some extras on hand if you want to add it on."

"I have the hairpiece," she said. "What is the total?"

"This order was prepaid. So you're all set." Diana smiled.

The woman smiled back but the conflicting emotions in her eyes said something was up. "Thank you," she said. And then she turned and left.

Ken felt like he was supposed to do something. At least get her name, her social media, some way to find out more about her other than she was from here and had the name Mei.

His aunt was staring at him with a knowing look. He changed his face to what he hoped looked like an innocent expression. In court, he was known for being unreadable. Good thing the rest of his family weren't lawyers.

"Give me one minute." She rushed out into the alley. He was prepared to give her more than a minute because the only thing he had scheduled for today was this. Or maybe catching up on work. So yeah.

He could swear he used to have hobbies or something before law school. He should probably make a note to figure out what they were.

His aunt rushed back in. "Davey! Davey!" She popped open one of the fridges and grabbed a box, expertly holding the one above it so it slid down and as she pulled the other out. "Davey, stop texting your boyfriend and get out here. Ken has to go."

"You know how to get to the Capitol, right?" Diana asked handing him the box.

"I do," he said, now thoroughly confused.

"Take these. She'll be there," Diana said.

"Are these for her?" Ken was confused. Hadn't they given her her order? Was she a tour group leader? Why would she be at the Capitol?

"They're for Kamehameha," Diana said. "You'll see when you get there. You have about an hour before the ceremony. Go!"

He took the box. He thought about asking if Kamehameha was the dead dude, but Diana was making shooing motions so he left. Instead of hobbies, right now he apparently accepted cryptic journeys from family members.

On the metro he googled Kamehameha. He was definitely dead, so Ken felt better about that. He had at least known that. June eleventh had been declared King Kamehameha Day back in the late 1800s in Hawai'i, but there was also a celebration in DC. Huh. People joked about DC being like a small town, and he absolutely did run into folks in the courthouse that he had some connection to all the time. But DC was also like thirty tiny villages sometimes. And you would discover two villages over they had been doing a thing your whole life that you had never heard of.

Today he was going to get a chance to see a new one.

EMANCIPATION HALL WAS part of the underground visitor's center that led to the US Capitol. It had a large white statue in the center. But today the focus was clearly over to the side. A large ladder was set up next to a statue of black and gold that Ken took to be Kamehameha I. Hula dancers and musicians were warming up. Chairs were lined up, some already filled with people.

It smelled like the musty air of old buildings, sweat, and his aunt's flower shop dialed up to eleven. The plain t-shirt and chinos he had put on this morning work well for the flower shop, but this atrium was a riot of color. There were Hawaiian shirts, floral sundresses, and flowers everywhere. People had flowers in their hair, around their necks, and many people seemed to have extras around their arms, like they needed to be ready to hand them off. Guitar music was playing. Even the Capitol Police guards stationed throughout the hall looked relaxed today.

He opened the box and inside rested three lei. One rose, one some sort of green leaf thing he couldn't identify, and one a pointier petal thing he also couldn't identify.

He pulled out the rose lei and put it around his neck. His aunt had said they were for Kamehameha, but he still didn't know what that meant.

He scanned the chairs and saw no sign of Ms. Mei, but decided to sit, not wanting to be in the way of whatever was about to happen.

The woman next to him pointed at his box. "If those are for him, you should go get in line."

Ken gave her a confused look and she pointed behind them, where there was a line of folks holding lei.

"Oh, but-" he started to say.

"Go on," she made a shooing motion.

Ken got up. He was really sure he was not supposed to be part of the ceremony. He looked at the line of people. Many of them wore matching outfits, hula costumes, Hawaiian shirts, or more generic button-downs. There was one person who didn't seem to match the rest of the line, so he made his way toward her. The groups seemed more likely to try to confirm what he was doing with someone else. He could hopefully hand off this box and move to the stairs or somewhere far away from anywhere he'd be asked to dance, perform or whatever it was that all these people were lining up to do.

"Hi, I think this is for you," he said shoving the box at her. Usually, people grabbed things you shoved at them in surprise and then you could carry on. He had learned that trick during a stint as a process server. But the lady turned to look at him.

"What are you doing here?" Ms. Mei asked.

"Oh," Ken said, his legendary ability to think on his feet disappearing in a puff of smoke. "Hi."

"Okay, folks," a woman with a clipboard said. "The Senator is going to say a few words and start us off, and then you can each process through with your offerings. Please just follow the folks in front of you and don't be precious about handing things over to Keoni on the ladder, okay? We'll all have time for chit-chat and stuff after the ceremony."

"You should take them out of the box," Ms. Mei said.

Ken knew the wise choice, the smart choice in this moment was to admit he was just here to watch, and to go sit down. But he wanted to learn Ms. Mei's first name. And this seemed like the only way today ended with him acquiring that knowledge.

This had turned into either Ken's worst idea ever or best idea ever. Really it depended on if he managed to get her name.

Several conch shells sounded at once. The crowd hushed and eyes turned toward the small dais set up next to the statue. A small woman, with rigorously styled black hair who Ken recognized as being one of the senators from Hawaii stood in front of the mike. "Aloha," she said. "Kamehameha the first, sometimes called Kamehameha the Great is credited with many things. One of the things I think that gets overlooked in his legacy is the Kanawai Mamalahoe or the Law of Splintered Paddle. I see many heads nodding so I won't bore you with the whole story. Kamehameha didn't invent the idea of what we now call humanitarianism, but he used his time as a leader to advocate for it. That is the spirit that we look to. Caring for others, and looking out for those whom the world has not properly provided for. I think that speaks to the spirit of Hawaii as I have known it, and what so many of us look for in each other and in our government today. Mahalo." The senator held up a lei on her arm and walked over to hand it to the dude on the latter. He used a large hook to raise it and place it over the statue's outstretched arm.

The lady with the clipboard gestured to the group at the front of the line and Ken watched carefully.

The first group processed forward in their coordinated outfits, chanting. The clipboard lady made no move to stop them so apparently this was expected. He wanted to ask Mei if you could just hand over the lei, but now that he was trying to act like he'd always meant to be there, he was going to have to do a lot of hoping.

The next group had one long lei spread out over several people's shoulders. Right, he had been told to have the lei ready. He opened the box and took out the lei. He still had nowhere to put the box so he just tucked it under his arm.

The line moved forward as the next group went. They processed quietly so Ken felt a little tension ease his shoulders. Many of the lei were super long and unconnected, so they dangled long from the statue's arm. The lei he had on his arm were all the connected circle type and didn't look as long.

He followed Mei down the aisle between the sets of chairs. Once they made it to the statue, Mei nodded and handed her lei to the guy with the hook.

Ken noticed her lei were extra-long. So apparently, he was the one with the wrong lei. But Mei looked over at him and smiled encouragingly, and he handed his lei to the guy with the hook. He watched him carefully, he didn't seem to give away anything with his expression that these were totally the wrong lei. The guy added them to the stack. Mei nodded again and moved away and Ken followed.

She took a seat in one of the chairs and there was a seat next to her. He slid into it and hoped this was a good sign.

Chapter 3

Jia had seen no sign of her mom. Just this flower shop guy. She wasn't sure what to think, but she guessed she had about seven hulas, two speeches, and eight songs before she could be expected to do anything. There weren't a lot of cultural Hawaiian traditions that occurred in DC. Many of the traditions her cousins who were still scattered across the islands participated in were a mashup - the Shinnyo Lantern Ceremony was based on Japanese Buddhist traditions, malasadas for Lunar New Year was a Chinese and Portuguese combination, even what mainlanders called Hawaiian bread was based on a Portuguese baking tradition.

As a Hawaiian born and raised on the East Coast, this was kind of it. This was the thing, other than classes at the local Hawaiian school, that her mom could bring her to every year to just be Hawaiian for the day. Her parents had met in Hawai'i when her dad was stationed there with the military.

Jia's mom had always wanted to own her own restaurant. When her parents had decided to move here, they thought the lack of existing Hawaiian restaurants was a plus. Also, her dad's family all lived in the area.

Jia couldn't remember her mom ever missing this ceremony. Not even the year that her parent's trademark lawsuit had made them national news. Her dad had skipped that year, of course, but he'd skipped several over the years. When her parents had run the restaurant together, they had always closed on this day. Had a small staff luncheon after the ceremony. Now that Dad ran his restaurant, they stayed open and offered Kamehameha Day specials.

But the divorce and everything that went with it had made it clear that her dad was a little more interested in adulation than he was in being a dad, or most likely a husband. That it wasn't so much that he hadn't liked the way her mom was running the restaurant, he had disliked the restaurant seeming like her thing that he worked at.

Jia: Mom, are you at the ceremony?

No sign her mom was texting back, which was normal. Her mom hardly ever checked her phone during the day.

She pocketed her phone and tried to pay attention to the hula. Jia had done hula at the same halau these students were from in Northern Virginia for about two years before she'd had to quit. The combination of tuition, plus the travel to Northern Virginia in rush hour traffic, right when the restaurant was gearing up for dinner had made it impossible. Watching these students now part of her wanted to get up and match their arm movements and steps. Good dancers made it look easy to pick up.

She applauded the dancers and they brought out a speaker. Jia fixed a polite expression on her face and wondered why her mom hadn't texted back. She pulled the phone back out and googled the restaurant. Yep, there was a note on there reminding customers that they were closed.

And her dad's restaurant had a big splashy reminder to come for the celebration. Bottomless Pineapple drinks. She shut the page down in the phone's browser.

Time to focus on something else. Next to her, the flower shop guy shifted. She tried to sneak another look at him with her peripheral vision. She hadn't paid enough attention to him at the flower shop. Only enough to be annoyed that he clearly didn't know enough to help.

But well, a big flower day, she likely should have expected that they'd be busy and gotten there earlier.

This event was partially sponsored by the Hawaii State Society, which contained a lot of people who like her dad were not of Hawaiian descent but had lived there and enjoyed the traditions. So it wasn't unusual for folks who possibly weren't Hawaiian to participate.

He was cute. Jia normally prized competence, but his confusion didn't seem to stem from not caring or not wanting to be good at his job, more from not having the training to handle the role he had been given for the day. Even now, he had the box he hadn't thought to get rid of tucked under his chair. He hadn't tried to toss it to the side, not caring who had to clean it up.

Flower shop guy shifted again. Jia noticed of the three lei he had had, he had selected the rose one for himself. The hairpiece she had placed in her hair as she metroed in had been treated with something so it would last. It matched the rose lei he was wearing. DC humidity wasn't always kind to flower lei. The flowers that were easy to find also differed from traditional flowers used in lei. So there were a lot of folks wearing kukui nut lei. Jia had broken one out herself that had cherry blossoms painted on it.

The last song listed in the program began, and Jia had not heard back from her mom. She was torn. Jia wanted to know if her mom was okay, but having conversations here was fraught. Too many of the folks her mom didn't want to know anything was ever wrong came to this event. In fairness, there were a lot of people here who said things like, "It's too bad it ended up in the news." Because yes, her parent's divorce being in the news was the sad part. Not her parents arguing over the restaurant, not her dad starting his own restaurant that he then named the same thing, trying to confuse customers and search engines, not the fact that his restaurant did every tacky catering to tourists thing that her mom had always refused to do, and not that both her parents asked her to testify against the other in court. It was really only sad that other people knew about it.

If Jia's mom wasn't here then maybe Jia didn't have to make small talk with anyone who would tell her something ridiculous about how she should feel. Jia could maybe talk to the flower shop guy. Jia couldn't remember the last time she had talked to a guy who didn't work in the food industry. It was probably when she had talked to one of her parent's lawyers, but that hardly counted. It might actually be college.

So, Jia was overdue for flirting. She was overdue for a lot of things. They applauded the final performance and folks all started standing and chatting.

She turned to the flower shop guy and held out her hand. "Hi, I'm Jia, I don't think I ever got your name."

Chapter 4

"I'm Ken." Ken shook her hand and trying not to think too hard about how her hand was soft and smooth. He wanted to do things he should definitely not be thinking about right now.

He wasn't sure why he was so taken. Jia was interesting. And maybe working long hours at the firm meant he met very few interesting people who weren't clients.

"So, weird question," Jia said, "Is this your first time at the ceremony?"

"That obvious, huh," Ken asked. He had thought he had at least faked it well enough to pass.

"No, but well, I've come every year, so I know most of the regulars, especially the ones who grew up here." Her face changed from a friendly interest to something barely polite. Before he could wonder too much about what he had said another voice spoke over his shoulder.

"Jia! So great to see you. Oh, sorry, this must be your boyfriend. Hi, I'm Bobbie, I've known Jia since she was born, so you come to me if you need embarrassing pictures or anything like that."

Ken turned to find a small white-haired woman in a red and white Hawaiian shirt and chinos. She patted his arm gently.

"I'm Ken," he said.

"Aloha, Bobbie," Jia said. She nodded but made no move to get past Ken. So he stood where he was, feeling like somehow his job for the moment was a protective barrier.

"Aloha," Bobbie said drawing out the word. "Well, I'm sure I'll see you later. Are you bringing your Ken to your dad's restaurant after this or are you doing something with your mom at hers?"

The gleam in Bobbie's green eyes spoke of data gathering, of huge meaning being assigned to the answer Jia gave. Ken may have known Jia's first name for a matter of minutes, but he suspected Bobbie's interest was not because she was concerned for Jia's emotional well-being.

"Oh my gosh," Ken said, his surprised voice quite believable if he did say so himself, "we should probably get going if we want to be on time, Jia." He held a hand out to her and was gratified when she accepted it. He looked back at Bobbie. "It was so nice to meet you."

He led Jia away. In the hallway, he realized he'd forgotten the box. "Shoot. I left the box. Let me go grab that. You can wait here. Or honestly, if I overreacted and you didn't need me to run interference, you could leave. No harm no foul."

"I can wait for you," she said.

Ken smiled. He walked back. He snagged the box and kept up the appearance of a harried person who must leave immediately.

Ken made it back to where Jia stood. She turned and followed him as he headed out. Now he had to figure out what they should do next. He wanted to talk to her in a place where she was neither in need of customer service nor fending off nosy family friends. A restaurant seemed like a good idea. Of course, her family seemed to own restaurants, so perhaps not. They were downtown on the Mall. There were always food trucks. Sometimes, on a weekend day, there were even good ones.

"So," he said as they stepped out into the hot June sun, "could I interest you in finding a food truck to grab something? I didn't eat breakfast this morning."

"Sure," Jia said.

He grabbed his phone, hoping his favorite food truck that sometimes stationed itself near his law firm was out today. Out today in walking distance even. Oh yes, the universe was working for him at the moment, because they were over by the Air and Space Museum today, which was super close.

He stopped on the sidewalk in front of the Take a Bao truck. Ken looked at Jia. "Mind if I order?"

"Go ahead," she said.

Ken smiled. "Can we get three duck, three portabello? Oh and two waters."

The server nodded and got to work on the order.

Jia looked at him. "Are the portabello or the duck for me?"

"I figured we could share unless you only want one kind, in which case I can eat the others," Ken said.

"Sharing sounds good," Jia said.

Ken paid for the order but noticed Jia slipped some cash into the tip jar. They walked over to the Mall. The benches nearby along the path all had people in them. The benches were long, some still with space, but Ken selfishly didn't want to share Jia. Jia reached into her purse and unrolled a scarf thing.

"We can sit on this," she said. She placed the scarf on the ground. It had a floral design and was long enough for each of them to sit without having to be in each other's laps. He handed her the box of bao.

Jia grabbed a duck and a mushroom bao. She moaned in appreciation and Ken felt pretty pleased. He found making her happy was a high goal for him. He selected one for himself and took a bite. Yeah, they were so good. He managed to resist moaning himself but mostly because he didn't want her to think he was teasing her. These bao were the lotus style of steamed and folded dough around the filling. Eating them with their hands was an easy experience, although Ken kept an eye on the filling to make sure no deliciousness disappeared.

After they finished eating their bao, Jia went for duck for her third, and Ken took the last mushroom.

"So you know where to find good food trucks, on the Mall even, any other special skills?" Jia said.

Oh wow. Ken discarded several responses that were probably too much for approximately an hour of knowing each other's names. "Well, I have been known to intervene in awkward situations, but I don't know if that's more of a hobby or a skill." His phone buzzed and he pulled it out.

Diana: No need to come back and help, by the way. I told your mom I needed you for a very special errand.

Ken: Thanks

"Everything okay?" Jia asked.

"Yeah," Ken pocketed the phone. "My aunt was letting me know she didn't need any more help today. It's her flower shop."

"Ah," Jia nodded. "Well, I happen to have today off too. Since you seem good at suggestions, what do you think I should do?"

"When was the last time you went to one of the museums?" Ken asked.

Jia looked out at the museums. "Probably school?

Ken looked, trying to remember which building was which museum. "And probably in school you went to both Air and Space and Natural History?"

"Is Natural History the one with the mammoth? Then yes, I have definitely been there."

"Let's try American History. Well, assuming I get to come with you."

"I would never abandon the guide that had gotten me this far," Jia said with a smile.

Ken wanted to kiss that smile. But well, perhaps they should see how much she liked his museum selection before he got cocky.

JIA WAS FINDING KEN a delightful distraction. She should be worried that her mom hadn't texted. But instead, she was playing hooky.

Her phone buzzed.

Mom: I'm fine, just resting today. No need to worry.

Jia paused.

Jia: Okay, I'll talk to you later.

Later would be, well, later. Her mom deserved rest, and Jia deserved things that were not work too. She really did have the rest of the day to play hooky with. It's possible considering hanging out with someone just for fun hooky was a sign that the apple didn't fall far from the tree, workaholic-wise.

Growing up in the restaurant industry, Jia had seen relationships that moved at the speed of light. Nothing was more embarrassing than having to work a shift next to someone you had awkwardly tried to hit on the night before. So she had stopped dating where she worked. Jia had certainly dabbled in the opportunities, in late-night hookups, and sometimes even repeated meetings.

But lunch? With a person she hadn't yet had sex with? But where the possibility lingered? It was a new thing for Jia. As was wandering into a museum in daylight, walking past crowds of tourists.

"There's a food exhibition I'd love to take a look at," Ken said, "but we can wander through on our way there."

Jia nodded. "Did you pick food because you heard my parents have a restaurant? Restaurants?" Jia was having fun with this idea that Ken knew so little about her life. The restaurant business always had people coming in and out of it. But having been a part of it one way or another for so much of her life, she met very few people who didn't have some ideas about her.

"I picked food because I like food. But if it's not your thing, you can pick another one and we can always meet up. Although then I'd need your phone number."

Jia smiled. "I have no objection to food." She also had no objection to giving Ken her phone number. But well, she knew how to be a little bit coy. Maybe.

Ken smiled back. He had a really good smile. She stopped in front of a shell necklace that the card said was an African shell. And she turned a corner to see mostly books. She liked books, but she suspected none of these were romances or other fun books. They had leather covers, next to staid photos. She picked up her pace, not interested in lingering when she saw a glimpse of one photo that felt familiar. She turned expecting to find a boring old president or something.

Chapter 5

I t was a woman, in black and white. She wore a stern expression and the hair and dress of the 1800s. Jia moved closer and read the tag. Her hand moved to her chest. The red leather book had gold script stating, "Hawaii's Story by Hawaii's Queen Lili'uokalani". Two words were surrounded by what looked like two tall torches and a crown atop a lei decorated the top. She had a copy of this book, at home. A worn paperback her mother had given her when she came home crying that the history teacher couldn't even pronounce Lili'uokalani's name.

"Oh cool," Ken said coming to stand beside her.

Jia nodded. She didn't know how to tell him how cool it was to see something from Hawai'i in a museum. The Museum of the American Indian briefly mentioned Hawai'i. But even her AP American History class textbook dedicated approximately two paragraphs to the annexation of Hawai'i. Most people talked about it wanting to become a state as if Hawai'i had just been slow to decide on statehood, overlooking that it hadn't even been part of the United States until a group of Americans decided it would simplify sugar trading if it was.

This was definitely not the kind of revelation one shared with someone one hadn't even kissed yet. "Take me to food," Jia said.

The food exhibit was fun, from kitchen setups to cookbooks, to looks at global influences on American cuisine. "I have that one," Jia pointed at one of the cookbooks in the display.

Ken smiled. "I don't have any cookbooks, is that a good one?"

"Well, do you know how to like boil water or whatever?" Jia asked. She had discovered even in the food industry you couldn't be sure. As long as you worked front of house somewhere that fed its employees on the regular, some people could get away with never learning. Jia had learned how to make every recipe they served in her mom's restaurant growing up. But now that she was front of house, she left much of the cooking to others.

"Of course." Ken scoffed. "I even know how to cook rice without a rice cooker. Although I do have a rice cooker."

"Do you use your rice cooker?" Jia asked. "And do you cook just rice in it, or other things too?"

"Oh, I hadn't realized we were at the interview portion of the day."

Jia shook her head. "Sorry, I do have a lot of thoughts about cooking."

"No." Ken reached out to rub her shoulder. "It's fine. I did ask. So, I only cook rice in my rice cooker. Am I missing out?"

"Well, no, because rice is amazing. You do have the option to use it for other things, but what do you usually do with the rice?"

"I work long hours so, I mostly just use it for something like a stir fry or fried rice. Or to replace the crappy rice I get with takeout."

"Well, you should stop buying takeout from places that can't make rice."

"I know, but they are right by my office, and it's just so easy," Ken said.

Jia wondered what office he meant. But she had already turned this into far too serious of a discussion. She had no interest in finding out what underpaid office drone job he worked at when he wasn't helping at his aunt's flower shop. She needed to turn this conversation back to something more likely to lead to her finding out what his lips tasted like.

Her phone buzzed.

Angela: Your mom wanted me to tell you everything's fine and she'll talk to you later this week.

"Everything okay?" Ken asked.

"Yeah," Jia said. Things were definitely fine if Angela said so. Or at least not terrible. "My mom's coworker says everything's fine. Sorry. I was checking on her because I thought she'd be at the ceremony. This used to be one of the few days of the year she wasn't working. So, thanks, I guess. For taking what could have been a weird day and making it interesting."

"Yeah, I made a change at work and my mom has decided this means that I don't have enough to do. So she keeps volunteering me for things, like helping at my aunt's flower shop."

"Oh, so that isn't your normal job?" Jia teased.

"No. I'm a lawyer," he said.

"Ah. Well, don't take this the wrong way, but I kinda hope you're a better lawyer than a flower shop employee." She should have guessed lawyer. The federal government kept a lot of lawyers in business in the area.

"Was I that bad? I mean obviously I couldn't find your order, but I got you help?"

"You did. But you got me help by leaving the entire front of the store unattended. I could have taken all the cash and been gone before you got back."

Ken put a hand to his face. "Guess that's why she was so willing to send me away." He chuckled. "Well, I am a better lawyer than that. I had been trying my hand at doing some mediation too, trying to help people get things resolved without having to bring a judge into it. But well, I had a case that went badly, and I took a step back from things. Like you said, obviously things go wrong and it isn't up to me to fix it. But, it's hard not to feel like I could have changed it somehow."

Ah, guilt over other people's relationships was far too familiar. "My therapist said my parents' relationship was their relationship, and my relationship with them is a separate entity. It makes sense like in theory. I even believe it most days. I just - everything they do now, everything they want to talk about is wrapped up in what happened. They both want me to work with them, but like I just can't."

"Because it feels like taking sides?"

"Oh, I did take sides. My dad went way over the line. But it doesn't mean my mom is perfect, or like that I wouldn't have gotten mad working for her. I guess that's part of it too, right? Like I get why they were frustrated with each other. They didn't just end their marriage, they made everything about the split this football. And I don't want their marriage footballs. That's such a weird metaphor. Does that make sense?"

"Yeah, it does. I'm sorry."

"You didn't do anything." Jia desperately wanted to get back to the flirty place, the fun place. "What made you pick the rose lei?" she asked. And well, if she looked at his lei, and the shirt-covered chest underneath it, well, that was just natural. She wondered what it would be like to touch the lei. Figure out a way to find out if his chest felt as solid as it looked. His arms and wrists were well-shaped, it made her more curious about the rest.

"I like red," he shrugged.

It was as good an answer as any. Maybe it was time to be bolder. She had no idea if dating non-restaurant folks followed the same rules anymore. But today had been about kings, queens, and remembered power.

"Maybe you should show me this rice cooker," she said.

Chapter 6

Ken had never thought of rice cookers as sexy or even flirtatious. But it looked like today was full of new things. "Is it okay if I kiss you first?" he asked.

She nodded.

Ken leaned forward, pressing his lips to hers, their mouths gently opening so their tongues could touch. It was a sweet kiss, it was a museum-appropriate kiss, and despite the cool museum air, he felt heat building in his blood. He pulled back afraid any more would lead to him doing something not museum appropriate, but he grabbed her hand squeezing it gently. Jia squeezed back and he smiled as he recited statistics in his head so he could manage to walk out of this museum without everyone who caught sight of him knowing what was on his mind.

He called for a rideshare once they made it to the sidewalk. They would have to change trains if they took metro, the bus ride was just not sexy, and he really wanted to move quickly. For all he knew she regularly asked to see people's rice cookers. He wanted, well, he wanted. He wanted her to see his rice cooker and whatever else she chose to see.

Inside the car, he grabbed her hand again, wanting to at least touch part of her. It seemed ridiculous. He had sat through meetings with multiple couples who dove in fast and then later discovered they didn't have enough in common to stick it out for the long term. And yet, here he was convinced that every new thing he learned about Jia would be just as amazing as the last.

"This is my building." He led Jia up to his apartment trying to remember if he had put his underwear away. He usually did, convinced his mother's all-seeing eyes knew whenever he didn't.

The place was what the rental agency generously referred to as a junior one-bedroom. There was a suggestion of separation between the area with his bed and the rest of the apartment. The open doorway to the galley kitchen was catty-corner to the main door. He kicked his shoes off near the door and waited as Jia did the same. He led Jia into the kitchen and with a flourish presented his rice cooker.

She looked at the rice cooker and back at him with a smile that stirred and heated his blood. "It's a very nice rice cooker. Do you want to save the lei?" She pointed at his lei.

"Sure," he said.

Jia nodded and removed hers, then his, opening his fridge door. She gently lay the lei on the empty top shelf.

Jia turned back and pressed her whole body against him. Their heights were close enough that chests, stomachs, and hips lined up together in delicious ways. Her lips and tongue met his, and as he kissed and tasted her, her hands moved over his back, untucking his shirt.

She pulled back, "May I?" she asked.

Ken nodded. She lifted his shirt off and the appreciative look in her eyes heated his blood even more. She moved to his pants, and he helped her get them undone and shucked off. He was grateful the boxer briefs had a reasonable amount of stretch since his cock was straining against it. But that could wait, because Jia still had all her clothes on. He led her around the edge of the kitchen wall, wanting to be near the bed before he helped her remove the shirt. She unclasped the bra, releasing her breasts. He wanted to touch but also didn't want to stop her as she moved to strip her pants, and then her panties, revealing her whole body.

He lifted her onto the bed. He leaned over her, soaking in this moment, trying to remind himself to be slow, to be methodical, that all the things he wanted would be better if he didn't give into the urge to hurry. His cock disagreed.

He kissed her lips, and her collarbone, feeling the change in skin texture. Learning the way her skin smelled. He stroked his hands over her breasts. "Anything off limits?" he asked.

Jia shook her head.

He licked each nipple, watching them peak in response. He ran his hands over her stomach and hips, the tops of her thighs, before dipping a finger over her clit and inside her. He stroked her clit with his thumb and then shifted so he could suck it into his mouth as he stroked two fingers inside her, feeling her clench around him as he increased the pressure and speed. He watched her face, watched her tip her head back as she tensed and came.

He licked her one more time. He shifted off the bed to shuck the briefs and grab the condom.

She sat up. "Let me." she reached for the condom.

"I'm so close," he warned but handed it to her.

"Good," she said with a smile. She opened the packet and smoothed the condom over his penis, swiftly, though he swore every light stroke of her fingers made him hotter. She lay back down spreading her legs wide. He moved back over her, leaning down to kiss her before he pressed inside her. He paused, feeling her stretch around him.

She reached her hand down to cup his butt, "Move, please." She shifted her hips against him, and he began moving, feeling the sensation build in his spine as his body moved against hers. He pinched her nipple and she gasped, clutching her hand tighter around his butt. She tilted her hips, shifting the angle and he could tell from how her thighs tensed that she was getting closer. He kept up the motion, the pressure, reminding himself to wait, to let her come first. She gasped and he felt her tighten further around him as she came. He kept thrusting, drawing it out as long as he could, but then it exploded inside him. He tried not to slump against her too hard as he finished, but that was as much thought as he had left at that moment.

JIA LAY ON THE BED feeling the sweat cool. She felt amazing and drained, satisfied, and hungry. She wanted more of this, of this man for sure. Ken returned from the bathroom and lay down next to her. She turned to look at him. Yep, even outside of the first-look sex haze, his body was solid and lean and made her want to stroke it.

Giving into the temptation she ran a finger down his chest. He grabbed her hand as it moved towards his belly button. "Gotta give me some time here."

Jia shrugged the shoulder that wasn't pressed into the mattress. "I was just exploring," she said.

"Uh-huh." Ken leaned forward and kissed her nose. "So let's talk logistics."

"Ugh," Jia said with a smile. Usually, she was the one requiring logistics discussions. Like yes, Tony, we could put cherry blossoms in every drink for the month of April. Have you priced out what it cost to buy a hundred cherry blossoms? And where are we going to put a hundred cherry blossoms? And how much does that add to the cost of the drink? Tony liked to call her the fun killer. So, yes, they should discuss logistics. "So, yeah, I should probably tell you I have to be at work tomorrow."

"I do not. I have some document review I need to do, but I have all day for that. What time do you need to be at work? Do you need to go home first? Because I am happy for you to stay," he said.

"You are happy to have more sex," Jia said wanting to be frank. It was easier to be clear rather than trying to pretend they had formed a soul-deep connection just because their bodies had bumped. Sure, he'd been surprisingly aware, surprisingly interesting, and well, unsurprisingly good in bed, but pheromones faded.

"That too," he said.

Jia's wardrobe was almost entirely black pants and black tops, with the occasional black dress thrown in for fun. If she showed up at work tomorrow in exactly these clothes, no one would know. It was easier to shower when she had her own hair gel, but she could let it dry in a twist. It would be hell to fix on Monday. But the restaurant was closed, so she'd have all day to get the tangles that putting it up still wet would lead to.

"I can use your shower, right?" It seemed implicit in the you can stay offer, but the whole point of reviewing logistics was to review logistics.

"Of course. As many times as you need," Ken said.

"Well, then, I guess I'm staying. Oh wait, how many condoms do you have?" she asked.

"More than we could use tonight," he said.

"Well that sounds like a challenge." Jia shifted closer, so her breasts pressed against his chest.

He pressed his lips to hers, and she pressed a hand on his hip, enjoying the feel of him everywhere.

"It wasn't a challenge. But we can certainly keep track of how many we use. Should we need that information again."

His hand slid between them and stroked between her legs. "That sounds like a plan," she said before he stroked again and she forgot how to speak.

Chapter 7

Jia texted her mom while she was metroing to work, hoping to catch her before Ko'u Keiki opened.

Jia: Do I need to call 911, mom?

Mom: What's wrong? Why would you need to call 911?

Jia: Because you didn't come to the Kamehameha ceremony. You sent me flowers and then weren't at the ceremony.

Mom: So dramatic. I'm working today. You said you didn't want drama. I figured you could go to the ceremony and then not worry about drama. Was it good?

Jia: It was great.

Her fingers hovered over the keys as she tried to figure out what to say next. She had wanted her mom there, but she wouldn't have talked to Ken if her mom had been there. She had looked forward to seeing her mom somewhere that wasn't the restaurant. But given the questions from people like Bobbie, she could hardly blame her mom for not wanting to be there.

When Jia had said no drama, she meant she was opting out of talking about the divorce. Not out of talking to her mom.

Jia: I'm sorry you felt you had to miss it.

Mom: I'm glad you had fun. That's all that matters.

She clocked in and took up her spot at the front desk. Jia managed to greet customers with a smile, and listen to Tony tell her stories, in English this time, of the more memorable customers she had missed Saturday.

They were in the lull between the first wave of early dinner seekers, and the later wave, when Jia looked up and saw her dad walking through the door.

Oh no. This was neutral ground. Neither of her parents were supposed to come here. "Hello sir, are you sure you are in the right place?"

"I am," her dad said. His smile was jovial. He was good at being jovial no matter the circumstances. "How are you doing, Jia?"

Jia looked hopefully at the door. No customers appeared to be about to enter and provide a helpful distraction. The next reservation wasn't for thirty minutes. This man standing across from her at the hostess stand would appear to the other customers in the room to be a customer - so walking away and slamming the door would seem rude. "I'm fine, Sir. How many will be dining here today?"

"Jia, can you take a break for five seconds? Tony, hi, can I chat with my daughter for a minute?" her dad asked.

Jia turned to warn Tony with her eyes.

"Of course," Tony said. "Jia, why don't you two step outside for a second."

She glared at Tony. Then Jia smiled and locked up the computer before stepping outside and moving down from the entrance.

"Dad, spit it out, and then go." Jia folded her arms, even though outside in the full June sunshine, one generally wished to keep one's body parts loose and separate. Sometimes the body language was more important than saving sweat. The restaurant was cold enough that Jia could feel each hair on her arm laying back down in the heat.

"So, Jia, I wanted to talk to you about work, actually." Her dad's smile was still jovial and friendly. He was such a nice guy, people kept telling her after the divorce. He was such a nice guy. So nice that he smiled when he suggested the same thing for the forty-second time. So nice that he filed paperwork trademarking the name of the restaurant for himself, not telling Jia or her mom until it was approved, until he opened his own restaurant using that name.

Jia didn't respond. He'd tell her faster if she just waited.

"So, yeah, I know you didn't want to take sides in the divorce." He paused again.

Jia kept her scoff inside. She had taken several sides.

"But I wondered if given your mom's plans to sell, you would consider coming to work at my restaurant now. I could pay you what Tony's paying you and it would be the food you love."

"Mom's selling?" Jia asked carefully. She hadn't heard that. Her dad would never lie about such a thing, Jia couldn't believe her mom wouldn't tell her.

"Oh," her dad looked sheepish. He loved happiness, but not messy emotions. "I thought she would have told you. The Hardy Group made her an offer."

The Hardy Group owned a consortium of restaurants up and down the East Coast. They owned both a pizza and a burger chain that had slowly been replacing a bunch of long-time restaurants in the area.

"I'm not going to come work at your restaurant," Jia said, because that was the only thing she was sure of at the moment. "Anything else before I get back to work?"

Her dad's shoulders sagged. "Well, the offer's open if you change your mind."

Jia nodded. When he didn't add anything she walked back into the restaurant. She held up a finger to Tony and went back and grabbed her phone from her cubby.

Jia: Dad says you're selling the restaurant?

She tucked the phone into her pocket. She took the hostess stand back over from Tony, waving off his questions. She pulled her phone back out and searched. There it was, on one of the local accounts. "Rumors say longtime staple Ko'u Keiki is closing down. You might remember Ko'u Keiki making national news when the two owners divorced-" Jia closed out the article before reading about other people's interpretation of her parent's divorce. Everyone focused on the name dispute, like that part mattered as much as the betrayal inherent within. Like haha, couldn't one of them have just picked a different name.

Jia had her own thoughts about the name of the restaurant. Hawaiian for my child, this restaurant was the neediest of siblings. Her dad's new restaurant was some sort of step-something or other, but trying to take that metaphor too far was probably something she should leave to a trained therapist.

Before Tony left, he stopped by the desk. "Everything okay, with-" he waved his hands. Tony also didn't like messy emotions.

"Yeah. He shouldn't be back," Jia said.

"Your family could always come to eat here. It would be great press."

Jia smiled. Tony was a natural at marketing. "I'll be sure to mention that to them."

"Fine," Tony rolled his eyes. "Text me if anything goes wrong." He waved as he left.

Jia's phone buzzed as she was packing up.

Ken: I just got more documents to review, so raincheck?

Jia: Yeah.

Jia had been caught up trying to figure out when she could try to see her mom, so now was as good as any time.

When she got off the metro near the restaurant, it was dark. There were no lights, no sign of anyone in the back. No one responded when she knocked.

Her mom's apartment was dark too. So Jia went home. Maybe tomorrow she'd get a straight answer from someone about what was going on.

Chapter 8

K en worried Jia had taken the raincheck thing personally.

But it seemed like the kind of thing they needed to discuss in person. She worked nights and weekends, which honestly he often did too. He had briefly dated one person after law school who was also a lawyer. When after six months they had managed to find only three partial shared days in common they had called it quits. It was too hard to learn enough about someone in small bursts of time to decide if they were worth making more of an effort.

His mom had tsked at him for that. "You people expect everything to be easy. Love is work. You're good at work, you just have to pick a person you're willing to work with."

His dad had nodded and said, "Eh, if he's anything like me he'll know right away when he sees them. Then he'll just have to convince them."

"Well he should look at more people then," his mom had said.

Ken had laughed and changed the subject. But, he felt like his dad had been right. Jia was worth the work. He just had to figure out the best way to convince her.

She had responded to the various texts he had sent throughout the week, but they had all been one word or one emoji responses. If her parents both had restaurants, food had to be a good tactic right? Besides who didn't like food? Everyone needed food, right?

Ken: Hey, could I bring you some fresh bao?

He added a picture of the truck.

Jia: <thumbs up emoji>

He made the order and watched his phone. She texted him the address.

Jia: I'm going to have like ten minutes. Sorry, but I am so hungry. I mean we have food here. Obviously. But I eat it every day.

Ken smiled. That was as many words as he'd gotten in days. Plus he was getting ten face-to-face minutes. Bao really were magical.

Ken walked over the few blocks, scanning the addresses.

Jia popped out of the door. "Hello, let's go over there for a sec." She pointed across the street. In front of a bank, there were two large cement flower beds, the sides of which were wide enough to sit on. "Food first, then talk?" Jia said.

Ken nodded. He handed her three bao, two duck, one mushroom. He'd gotten the same for himself. He'd eaten lunch on a call today, so the bao disappeared quickly.

When he looked, Jia's were also gone. She wiped her hands with a napkin she must have already had.

"Sorry," Jia said. "And well, sorry I haven't responded much. My mom - well, something's going on with my mom and that's taken up a lot of the non-work time. I appreciate you being patient about all this."

"My schedule's kind of crazy too. I get it." Ken looked over. Jia was in all black again. No flowers in her hair, no lei, but she still stood out. "Is your mom okay?"

"Yeah. I mean she's telling me everything's okay. But I never know how much of that is true and how much of that is her protecting me."

"Oh yeah. My dad had a heart attack a few years ago, he's fine now. But when my mom called from the hospital, she was like everything's fine, I don't want you to worry. And I was like, well, if you are in the hospital things are by definition not fine."

Jia smiled and nodded. "Yeah, like that." She glanced across the street. "Okay, I hate to like eat and run, but we have a huge party coming in in like fifteen minutes, so I gotta get back. Thank you for feeding me. And I go back next week to having Monday and Tuesday off. Or, like Wednesday through Friday I don't work until four, so I could like have lunch? Office people still get lunch right?"

Ken smiled. "We do get lunch. What if we plan to meet Sunday evening - your place, my place, whichever works."

"For all you know, I live way out in the suburbs."

"Do you live way out in the suburbs?"

"No. I'll text you the address. Thanks again." She leaned really close. "I'd kiss you, but like three of my coworkers are staring at us right now and I do not want to reward their ogling. Raincheck?"

Warmth spread through Ken's chest. He wanted to touch her, to pull he closer, co-workers be damned. But he didn't. "Raincheck," he said. He watched her walk back across the street and pause to wave before she went back inside. He probably needed a cold shower. But instead, he'd go back to his industrially cool office and get some more reading done.

Chapter 9

K en stood outside the restaurant in a button-down shirt and dark slacks. Jia wanted to run her hands over those buttons, to rumple those slacks, and okay, maybe, it was a little warm out here already.

She grabbed Ken's hand, tugging him down the street, worried that things like hugging him might distract her from the getting him back to her place.

"Hi," she said to Ken as they waited to cross the street.

"Hi," he said. She could feel his eyes on her and she turned and looked. He kissed her. Lips quickly touched and then he tugged her across the street.

"Last train dude, stop distracting me." She smiled because she liked the distraction, but further delays to the time when they were somewhere private were not helpful.

Ken kissed her ear on the metro escalator. He gently stroked her arm on the metro platform. He placed his hand on her knee on the metro train. Jia had never been so grateful to be only five stops from home. To have an apartment right near the stop.

Each of these touches lit a tiny part of her on fire, such that she wanted to do something anything to get them somewhere faster. She fumbled for her security card, tugging Ken down the hall into her studio apartment. She had gotten all the laundry and the coffee mugs cleared away this morning. She had put fresh sheets on the bed and placed the box of condoms on the bedside table in easy reach.

As the door shut behind Ken, Jia pressed him up into the door, kissing him, running her hands down his chest.

Jia had missed Ken. Missed the way he smelled. She hadn't realized until she pressed up against him, feeling their skin touch that she could recognize how he smelled. How weird. And nice. His hand trailed down her side and that was even nicer.

She rolled him onto his back, pressing kisses to his collarbone, his stomach. She wrapped a hand around the base of his penis, looking, up, watching his eyes and she flicked her tongue over the head. She licked it from base to tip before sucking it inside her mouth. He groaned and placed a hand on her head.

"Please," he said, "I want to come inside you."

She sucked his cock one last time, but shifted, accepting the condom from him, and sliding it over him. She took him inside her. He clasped her hips. "Hang on a sec," he said.

Jia laughed. "You're kind of being a control freak here."

"I'm sorry," Ken said. "I can shut up."

Jia smiled. "What was your suggestion?"

"Can I?" He reached between them and began stroking her clit, rubbing it. Jia felt the pressure build and squeezed him tighter. She huffed and he increased the pressure, still keeping a hand tight on her hip, encouraging her to stay still while he worked. When she felt her thighs and spine tightening with building pressure, he relaxed his hand. Jia began thrusting. Ken's hand stayed between them so that she rubbed against it with each motion.

She came, feeling the room brighten and darken. She kept moving, thrusting through the aftershocks, feeling Ken's hips thrust against hers, and then he came.

After he got up, and Jia pointed to where the bathroom was so he could discard the condom.

She lay on the bed, basking in the boneless and relaxed sensation. It felt deeper than the that was a great orgasm relaxed. It felt like when you're tasting a dish and it's good, but suddenly, one more dash of spice and it crosses from good into sublime. Maybe she was just hungry. Because attaching your happiness, your sense of home to any one person was just not good. Not allowed. Not safe.

Ken wandered back from the bathroom. He paused in front of the side table she had an array of pictures on. Most of them had been in her parent's living room until the divorce. Framed pictures of her parents with her as a baby, her parents with her as a kid on the first day of the restaurant, her high school graduation, and her parents and her at the halau when they had the hula presentations.

He held up one of the pictures, his expression serious. "This is you with your parents?"

Jia got up and crossed, even though, the answer was obviously yes. She wanted to know which picture meant the night was moving to serious face, instead of let's hydrate before we have more sex face.

It was the picture of her high school graduation. Her parents had argued that day. But when the school photographer came, they gathered up and smiled. She loved and hated that photo. They looked happy, but it wasn't very real.

"Yeah."

"Your parents are Jeff and May Chapman?" he asked.

Jia nodded. Did he recognize them from the lawsuit? Jia's mom hadn't given any interviews, had said trying to win over the press was her dad's tactic, and May Chapman was going to trust the process.

Ken placed the picture frame back on the table. He pressed his fingers to his nose.

"I thought your last name was Mei?" Ken said.

"I go by Mei now. It's my middle name. After," Jia waved her hands, "everything, it was just weird. Especially trying to find a restaurant job. They all wanted to talk to me about the case. Tell me what they thought. Who they sided with. As if it was just a fascinating TV show, and not like my life. So I started going by Mei."

Jia felt leaden. Her toes pressed into the parquetry floor. She wanted to ask what was going on. She was sure she was going to hate the answer.

"So, it's weird," Ken said with a smile that looked more like a grimace. "I think we skipped over some things. Did I tell you I work in family law?"

Jia shook her head. Did he want to discuss the intricacies of her parent's case now? Because Jia had talked to plenty of people. Been advised that the court came to a totally reasonable decision when it decided that it was fine that her father had filed for a trademark of a name of a restaurant clearly conceived by her mother. That it was fine that he had registered for it using only his name. That it was fine that he used that to open a restaurant with almost the same name. That he had left out the 'okina or apostrophe when he filed, just meant that he was in the right to name his restaurant that. Sure, search engines couldn't tell difference between kou and ko'u even though in Hawaiian one meant your and one meant my. Even in his misspelling, her dad had revealed whose idea this was.

Then, after two years of court fees, her dad had oh so magnanimously changed the name of his restaurant to Na Keiki. So that now when you googled his restaurant you just got the restaurant website and related news. And when you googled her mom's restaurant, you got stories about the lawsuit.

"I was in training to become a mediator. As part of that, they assign you several cases with a mentor, and then several on your own."

Jia flexed her toes against the floor. Anything to ground her, to distract her, to remind herself that this was fine. It was time to rip off the bandaid. No need for a slow peel. "You mediated my parent's case," she said. She had met both her parent's lawyers of course. But the mediation the court had suggested at the start, well, from what she heard it had been great until her father announced his restaurant. And then the mediator had told them it seemed mediation would not be successful.

"Yeah," Ken said.

KEN HAD TAKEN ETHICS in law classes. They had discussed things like no matter what pop culture told you, you could not sleep with your client and still be their lawyer. But he was pretty sure they had never covered what happened if you discovered the person who was quickly becoming one of the most important people in your life, was part of the case that haunted you.

Of course, he knew things were strained with Jia and her parents. But somehow this particular possibility had not occurred to him.

"Okay," Jia said. "So what does that mean? Do you have thoughts on my parent's marriage or divorce or restaurant situation? Because if you do, you can keep them to yourself. I lived it."

"I can't discuss any of it anyway, not without your parent's permission. But, I'm sorry. I haven't mediated any cases since then. I just," Ken struggled to explain. He had made a suggestion that had spiraled out of control. His mediation mentor had told him that people who want to screw over their spouses do it with or without help. Suggesting Mr. Chapman offer to buy out the restaurant to run it himself had not made him start his own restaurant. And it had certainly not meant he needed to name it the same thing as his wife's. But all of that was case details. "I misread the situation and kept trying to resolve it, instead of turning it over to either a more experienced mediator or the lawyers sooner."

Jia moved past him. She gathered up the clothes on the floor near the door, placing hers into a pile on the couch. His she handed to him.

Ken wished he had kept his mouth shut. It was likely her parents barely remembered the mediator through the haze of bitterness they had been operating in. Ken was usually good with words, but they were all deserting him now. "This doesn't change how I feel about you. I just thought you should know."

"You thought I should know. My parent's case changed your life, is that what you're saying?"

"Well, no. But it did make me take a step back and consider whether mediating divorce was something I should be doing." He knew how weak that sounded as soon as he finished saying it. His mouth was still trying to fix it, get her to listen. But he could tell it hadn't helped. It had possibly made things worse.

"Cool story." Jia's arms were folded in front of her. "Because my parent's divorce changed my whole life. But I'm glad it gave you a learning opportunity. Since you like learning, I'm sure you'll figure out how to get home now." She pointed towards the door.

"Please, Jia, can we talk about this?" When she hadn't immediately kicked him out, he had been hopeful, but that hope dwindled.

"No, we can't," Jia said. "Please just go."

Her voice cracked and he decided that as much as he wanted to stay, to comfort her, to hold her, he needed to go. He put on his clothes. Doorknob in hand, he looked back. "Please call me tomorrow. We can figure this out."

She shook her head and pointed at the door. He left. He touched the door as it swung shut, waiting until he heard her turn the lock on the other side before figuring out how he was going to get home.

Chapter 10

Jia's coffee was defective. She was sure that was the reason she was dragging this morning. Unable to dig up motivation even though it was noon already. She decided to go visit her mom and have a conversation. Because if the day was going to be full of bad things, then they might as well pile them on.

Jia had no regrets about shoving Ken out the door in the middle of the night. She gave him his clothes after all. But the sad look on his face kept showing up in her head, and she wanted to punch things.

She metroed to her mother's apartment, ignoring the fact that she passed Ken's stop. It wasn't Ken's stop after all. She had lived her whole life up until now, not knowing Ken had existed prior to a few weeks ago. Soon enough she'd be back to thinking of the stop by its correct name.

Her parents' divorce had helped hone her skills when it came to getting used to things that sucked.

Jia didn't think she could have prevented her parents' divorce. She didn't think the lawyers or even the mediator could have fixed it. She did think her parents could have found a solution that wasn't national news. But Jia had been slowly building a life separate from her parents. A life that didn't involve anything connected to what either of them were doing. Sure, she gone back to the restaurant business. Jia wasn't trying to erase her entire life. But she wasn't working for any restaurant her parents owned or worked at. So sleeping with someone involved in their case was just too close.

It had been hard enough finding a restaurant that needed her and wasn't run by someone her parents used to work with. Tony had many faults, but his recent arrival in the DC restaurant scene had made him a perfect owner for her to work with.

Jia buzzed herself into her mom's building, knocking on the door with two coffees in hand.

"Jia? Did you tell me you were coming?" her mom asked.

"No, I'm a delightful surprise," Jia smiled. Based on her mom's face it seemed like the smile hadn't been very convincing. But her mom gestured to let her pass.

Jia toed off her shoes and went to sit at the small round table in the living and dining room. She gently pushed the stack of envelopes to the side before putting the coffees down.

"I got you coffee, Mom."

Jia's mom came and sat in the chair, sniffing the coffee. "Isn't it too late for coffee?" But she took a sip.

Jia sipped hers. "So tell me about the Hardy group."

"The Hardy Group? They own many restaurants. Why are you asking me this?" her mom said.

"Are you selling to them?" Jia asked.

Her mom wasn't able to cover the look of surprise. "Where did you hear that?"

"Why wouldn't you tell me you were closing the restaurant?" Jia asked.

"You said you wanted nothing to do with either restaurant. I assumed that included whether or not I sold it." Her mom stood. "Do you need something to go with this coffee? Did you eat lunch?"

Jia hadn't eaten lunch but she was more worried about not finishing this conversation. Her traitorous stomach growled.

"I'll get you food," her mom said. Her mom moved over to the fridge, pulling out containers.

Jia stood on the other side of the pony wall that separated the kitchen from the living room. "Did they give you a good offer or are you sick?"

Jia had disavowed herself of both her parent's restaurants, but she had also assumed that both of them would continue on, in perpetuity. Somehow.

"I'm not sick. I'm healthy as a horse. But I'm tired. I'm just tired, Jia." Her mom's back was to her, as she pushed a plate into the microwave.

"I'm sorry, mom, I know the restaurant was your baby."

Her mom turned and handed her a plate with two manapua. "You are my baby. The restaurant was a thing that I did. The Hardy group offered me enough money to close out the debts and pay the staff. And then I can figure out what to do next."

Jia's eyes filled with tears and she blinked trying to hold them back from spilling over. She took the plate. Gathering up the first bun in her hand she paused to inhale. The smell of curry chicken and apples wafted up. She took a bite. Her mom sat back down at the table with her.

When she had finished, her mom said, "So tell me about this boy?"

"What boy?" Jia asked.

"Pfft, you forget I still know people in other restaurants," her mom said.

"Are you getting people to spy on me?" Jia asked. She was sort of fascinated. DC often operated like a small town, especially within an industry like restaurants. But really, people were reporting to her mother that she had been seen with a boy? Jia wasn't sure how she felt about that. Especially since she had kicked said boy out.

Her mother was selling the restaurant that had been part of their lives for so long. It was both happy and sad. So few restaurants got to end on their own terms. Without a mountain of debt.

But her mom hadn't had more than three days off since they went to tutu's funeral, so this was also good. Her mom would get to rest. Get to do something else. And her dad would think she was coming to work in his restaurant, but she was going to stick with Tony for now.

And Ken?

"I am not getting people to spy on you," Mom said. "But also, if you wanted to be secret maybe don't be making out on the metro platform. Not judging, just stating."

Jia smiled. "Fair point. I don't know if he is - we - well things got messy," Jia said.

"Relationships are messy. If you want to fix it, you try. Food helps."

"You think food fixes everything," Jia said.

"Not everything. But most."

Chapter 11

Three of Ken's clients asked him if he was doing okay. Considering most of his cases involved divorce, it was a bad sign that his clients were worried about him.

He had replayed his conversation with Jia multiple times. Trying to figure out how he could have approached the conversation better. He had spent weeks after the Chapman case had made the news, trying to figure out if there was something he could have said or done to keep the situation from spiraling out of control.

His mentor had told him you can only work with the information you have. That family law wasn't for the faint of heart and he could go do something like tax law if he wanted a simple life.

Ken knew that. He knew the JD didn't come with magical powers, or make him better at solving things.

He had known the Chapmans had a daughter. Many of his clients did. Ken had never been naked with one of his client's kids, never kissed or stroked them, never watched them moan in delight at eating good food.

He was part of something she clearly wasn't over. He wasn't over it either. And one thing he had learned from his time working with families, is that you couldn't trump emotion with logic. If she wasn't over her parent's divorce, then it didn't matter if he had handled everything brilliantly or not. He was inextricably linked with that event for her.

He couldn't blame her for never wanting to see him again. He just didn't know what logic to use to tell his own heart that it was hopeless.

Chapter 12

Jia: Can we talk?

Jia pressed send and frowned at her phone. Can we talk was like the worst thing to ever text anyone. But hopefully, Ken would accept it as a small upgrade from please leave my sight immediately.

Having talked to her mom she had realized perhaps she had been a smidge hasty. She still had no regrets about kicking Ken out. But perhaps she could have done a better job considering that if her parent's marriage was destined to derail, he could hardly be faulted for having been on the train.

Ken had agreed to meet her near his office. They found a bench in the park across the street from his office and sat. Jia held the bag her mom had given her in her lap.

"I should warn you, my family is a mess," Jia said.

"Families always feel like a mess when they are yours," Ken said.

"Yeah, my parents." She took in a deep breath and then let it out. "My parents always fought, often at top volume. But like they always fixed it. My dad had big ideas, tons of them, and always wants to try or do the next thing. My mom moves more slowly. So they disagreed a lot. But they also seemed to balance each other out. So like, there'd be a big night of yelling, and then two days of curt words, and then I'd find them canoodling somewhere, back to being embarrassingly lovey-dovey."

Ken nodded. "My parents are - well, my mom says I shouldn't be embarrassed since that's why I exist, but yeah, finding my parents making out somewhere is not an uncommon thing."

Jia nodded. "So when they told me they were getting a divorce, I half expected it to just get fixed. Like sure, okay guys. But it didn't. And then it got worse than them just splitting up. The restaurant became the thing they kept fighting over. And the whole trademark thing. I usually handled all the paperwork for the restaurant. But I didn't even know my dad had filed a trademark for the restaurant name. Most restaurants don't. You only need it if you're creating a chain or something. Well, anyway, that's not the point."

Jia looked over at Ken. He was listening. He was letting her explain the law to him when he was a lawyer. That had to mean something. Hopefully.

"Anyway, when I found out about the trademark stuff, I told both my parents I was having nothing to do with either of their restaurants. Finding out you were part of it, it threw me. I reacted badly. You could have just not told me."

Ken shifted. "I met with both of your parents several times. It's possible they don't remember me anymore, but it seemed likely. But yeah, I probably could have waited until daylight to tell you."

"These are manapua. My mom made them. She's better at cooking, I do front of house and admin for a reason."

Ken opened the bag and leaned in to sniff them. "Are these a peace offering or a goodbye?" he asked.

"I'm hoping the first," Jia said keeping her whole body still. She wanted to look away, to not have to look at him as he answered, but it was too important for her to do that.

He reached down and handed one of the manapua to her. "Then how about you eat this one."

Chapter 13

Three months later

Ken waited in front of the restaurant for Jia. As the door shut behind her, Jia saw her dad standing just behind Ken. She grabbed Ken's hand. "Hi, Dad. We're on our way to-"

"The school, I know," Dad said. "Could you give your mom this? You don't have to say it's from me."

Jia accepted the box. It looked about the size for a lei, and the chilled cardboard plus the name of Ken's aunt's flower shop made Jia pretty certain of it. "You could give it to her yourself," Jia said.

Her dad shook his head. "No, I'd be a distraction from her day. But thanks. Maybe I can take you two to dinner sometime soon?"

Jia glanced at Ken. "Yeah, we'd love that. Text me."

Her dad nodded and then waved before he walked away. They were still figuring things out, Jia and her dad. He had stopped asking her to come work at his restaurant. Now they were trying to figure out how to be an adult kid and dad who did not have the same workplace.

At the halau, things were noisy and boisterous. Her mom had been added to the faculty as a food teacher. Kumu Chapman would lead the kids through a history of food traditions, explaining the various influences on Hawaiian food.

"Mom, they are so lucky to have you. Also, Dad wanted me to give you this," Jia handed over the box.

Her mom opened it, nodded, and placed the lei - one lily and one ti leaves - on top of the one the Halau kids had already presented her with.

Jia and Ken took her mom out for dinner after the welcome ceremony was completed.

On their way back to Ken's apartment, Jia leaned her shoulder on his head again. "I love you," she said. "Just thought you should know."

"I love you too," Ken said, patting her knee. "My parents have been asking when they get to meet you."

"Your parents have got to be less chaotic than my parents."

Ken squeezed her knee. "Let's hope you still feel that way after you meet them."

She did.

Acknowledgments

For DC area folks, I have somewhat fictionalized the DC Capitol lei draping ceremony for my own nefarious purposes. It is much easier to show up and just watch than I have portrayed it, I just couldn't resist. My writer brunch crew is great at saying yes, go write that every time I have a new idea. I haven't thanked any of my knitter crews yet, and well, they deserve thanks for keeping me entertained, giving me and excuse to knit for long stretches of time, and also, invariably talking about books.

It's also worth noting that the lei draping doesn't always occur exactly on Kamehameha Day, I just decided to streamline and make it a year where it fell on a Saturday and made the logistics easier.

Also, my local friends, I wish there was a local Hawaiian restaurant, much less two. Someday. Someday.

Many thanks to the beta readers who provided early feedback on this. Thanks to the Hawai'i State Society and other local Hawaiians who worked to both document and make this small bit of Hawaiian tradition accessible. The diasporan Hawaiian experience is always a weird experience of feeling a little disconnected even when in the exact spot you grew up in. These traditions, even though they bring up complex feelings about monarchies, are a touchstone that helps remind folks we are still here, we still exist. And having a local halau is not something I could have ever imagined growing up. Mahalo nui to all those working to keep those of us here connected, and provide opportunities for the curious to learn more.

Also reviews are always so important, please consider leaving one on your site of choice.

Also By Tara Kennedy

Bait Girl – A Young Adult Short Story

City Complications Series – Adult Contemporary Romance:

Aloha to You –Novella

Undercover Bridesmaid –Novel

Hot Bartender –Novel

City Entanglements Series: Adult Contemporary Romance:

Repeated Burn – Novella

Bored by the Billionaire – Novella

Clear as Ice – Novella

Not an Ending – a bonus epilogue available to newsletter subscribers

Of Kings and Queens - Novella

Non-Fiction:

Let's Talk About Fictional Sex

Find info on where to buy them at www.tarakennedy.com/books[1]

---

1.   http://www.tarakennedy.com/books

About the Author

Tara Kennedy was born and raised in Washington, DC. By day she wrangles bureaucracy and by night she writes tales of folks smooching and trying to forge their way in this world. Tara also knits, reads, watches TV, and drinks lots and lots of tea. She is trying to break a Twitter habit.

You can find more at www.tarakennedy.com

www.ingramcontent.com/pod-product-compliance
Lightning Source LLC
Chambersburg PA
CBHW061639130726

47996CB00003B/1367